PEN PALS

D1321864

PEN PALS

Edgar J. Hyde

CCP

© 1997 Children's Choice Publications Ltd

First published 1997
Reprinted 1999

Text supplied by Joan Love

ISBN 1 90201 201 1

Printed and bound in the UK

Contents

Chapter 1

"Natasha Morris, will you please tell me, and the rest of your classmates, what on earth is so interesting outside?"

With a jolt, Natasha turned towards the teacher.

"I'm sorry Miss Harrison, I was just thinking about . . ." Natasha's voice tailed away.

She couldn't think of an excuse, and she couldn't possibly tell the truth – that this morning's long winded history lesson bored her senseless! After all, wasn't history supposed to be about Henry VIII and his six wives, romance, divorce and gory beheadings. Instead she was having to sit and listen to two hours about crop rotation! Crop rotation – who on earth cared?

"No. Don't even bother stuttering your way through an excuse, just do me a favour and pay attention. Remember you've got an exam coming up next week, and crop rotation just might be one of the questions!" Miss Harrison turned to the rest of the class. "Now, where we?" Her voice droned on and on.

Olivia turned and smiled at Natasha sympathetically. The two were best friends, and had been since they first met up as four-year-olds in the same nursery. They were now in their first year of high school, enjoying feeling all grown up, carrying their books from class to class round the massive, never-ending corridors, giggling as they frequently got lost only to arrive red and breathless at their next class. They had made new friends too, there was Ellis, with her dark curly hair and large brown eyes. How Natasha envied her looks. Then there was Marcie, though Natasha couldn't quite make up her mind about her just yet. She was the complete opposite of Ellis, pale with long, strawlike blond hair and rather on the quiet side. "Pale and interesting, I suppose, if one was being kind," thought Natasha.

She hastily scribbled a note, "Meet you outside the library at four," and passed it deftly to Olivia without Miss Harrison noticing. Olivia quickly pushed the note inside her notebook and gave no sign of having received anything.

Natasha looked at her watch. Ten minutes past four. Where on earth had Olivia got to? Just then, she saw Olivia, Marcie and Ellis wind their way up the long path from the front of the school.

"You took your time," she smiled as all three girls stopped just beside her.

"Sorry, Natasha, my fault," said Ellis. "I left my new lipstick in the loos and had to go and rescue it – never know who you might see on the way home."

Ellis was always experimenting with lipsticks and eyeshadows, always on the lookout for free samples and arriving in school after lunch simply drenched in perfume, having just spent the best part of her lunch hour in the perfume department of the nearest store!

"You should try some, Marcie, look – it's

quite a pale pink, it'd look really nice against your complexion."

"Gosh, no," said Marcie. "My mum would have a fit – she says there's loads of time yet to put all that 'muck', as she calls it, on your face. Anyway, I'd rather keep my money for important things. I'm going to buy some new CD's at the weekend, at least they won't wear out like your make-up will!"

"Hey, Ellis," someone shouted from behind them. The girls turned to see Scott Gregson almost opposite them. He was the best looking guy in their year, and everyone but everyone had their eye on him. "If you're going home, I'll walk with you."

Ellis smiled. "See what the 'muck' on your face does for you girls!" she muttered. "Sure, Scott, I was just saying goodbye to the girls – see you tomorrow everybody." And off she went, pink lips glistening, dark curls bouncing, school bag slung casually over her arm.

"Don't you just wish you had her confidence," sighed Olivia.

"Yes, and her hair and her teeth and her eyes," replied Natasha. "Never mind, 'Make the best of what you've got,' is what my mother always says. Now let's see, what could you make out of us three."

And as the three started to wind their way home, they laughed together, picking out the parts of each other that they thought were the 'best bits'.

"Okay, Natasha," said Olivia "you give me your teeny tiny waist, Marcie can give me her small perfectly formed feet, I can probably get away with using my own hands – if I paint my fingernails – and, with the help of a wig, there we have it, the perfect Barbie doll!" "

And so the conversation carried on until the girls were almost home.

"Oh, and Natasha," Olivia began, "next time you write me a note in class, you really don't have to write my full name on it – I do know who I am!"

Natasha looked at Olivia quizzically, "I didn't write your full name, Olivia, in fact I didn't even write your first name!"

"Yes, you did," Olivia laughed, as she fished in both jacket pockets for the note. "You wrote, 'Olivia Goulden, meet you outside the library at four.' Blast, I can't find the note – oh, look, here it is."

They had now reached Marcie's house and Olivia had emptied the contents of her school bag on to the pavement outside. She showed the hastily scrawled note to Natasha and, sure enough, Olivia's name was written just above what Natasha remembered writing.

"That's really weird, Olivia, I don't remember writing that, it doesn't even look like my handwriting."

"Marcie, where have you been?" the girls heard Marcie's mum shout from an upstairs window.

"Oops, got to run girls, Mum wants me to go to the supermarket with her today – see you tomorrow."

"Sure, bye, Marcie," called the two girls as she disappeared inside her front door.

Natasha was still staring at the note. "Go on Natasha, stop trying to be funny. I mean if you passed the note straight to me, and I didn't add my own name to it, then who did?" Olivia protested. "Anyway, look, I have to run too, I'm baby-sitting Mrs Winter's twins tonight and I have to try and get my homework done before I go. I'll see you tomorrow."

"All right," sighed Natasha, "but I still don't understand."

She left Olivia at the end of the street where the road leading to her house forked left.

Weird, she thought, she must have been in more of a bored stupor than she realised this morning. How could you write someone's name and not remember?

"Suzanna Craigson," she read aloud from one of the gravestones in the cemetery. She had to pass the cemetery every day and night going to and from school and, though was never comfortable with this, she found the best way round it was to make up stories about the people lying beneath the rows and rows of tombstones. That way it seemed to take the scariness out of things.

"Born 2 November 1906, cruelly taken from her beloved parents 1 November 1920."

Natasha had never noticed that particular stone before, or maybe it was just that she had never actually realised how young Suzanna had been when she died.

"Just a year older than I," she thought. "Wonder what happened to her."

The use of the word 'cruelly' seemed to indicate murder or something gory and horrible.

"Better stop thinking about it," she decided. "Mum always says my imagination's too vivid – it'll end up getting me into trouble one of these days."

"Here comes fatso, here comes fatso."

Her young brother's chanting soon stopped her daydreaming.

"Come here, Tommy, you little brat," she laughed, chasing the bubbly little three year old into the back garden. "I'll give you fatso."

She grabbed the little figure and hugged him tightly round the waist, lifting him right off his feet. She kissed him loudly on the lips and came away covered in green sticky stuff.

"What have you been eating now?" she smiled.

"Gooey monsters," he said and showed her the empty packet.

"Green Slimey Guts," she read aloud. "Made from jelly and packets of sugar and full of additives," she added, "your teeth will fall out," and poked him in the tummy playfully.

"Don't care about teef," he retorted. "Like gooey monsters!"

How did the rhyme go, she mused as she went inside to change. Sugar and spice and all things nice, oh yes, frogs and snails and puppy dogs' tails, or something like that anyway. Tommy was that, all right, and she adored every last little inch of him. She wondered if Suzanna Craigson had had a brother?

Chapter 2

Next morning Natasha simply couldn't believe they were having to play hockey outside in the muckiest conditions she had ever seen. It had started to rain last night and had hardly let up from then until now so that the pitch was virtually unplayable! Their gym teacher, however, had insisted that they don their gear and, "get on out there, gels – a bit of rain never hurt anyone!" So there they were, trying desperately to hit the puck into the opposing goal, but usually ending up sprawled on the ground with sticks and legs flying every way but the right way! She sidled over to where Olivia was standing on the pitch. Both Olivia and Marcie hated sport of any form and were both trying to look small and insignificant so that Miss Starrs wouldn't notice they were taking no part in the game!

"Managing to get away with it so far, then?" she hissed to the pair.

Olivia raised her eyes heavenwards, "I'm so wet and dirty I'll have to soak in a hot bubble bath for at least three hours tonight!"

Natasha laughed. Just then, one of the girls at the far end of the pitch started to run towards them. As she drew nearer, Natasha realised that the girl was Ellis, wearing a brand new bright orange and green headband. Ellis drew her stick back and swiped the puck as hard as she could.

The puck seemed to be heading straight for Olivia. Natasha moved forward to try and stop it but, to her surprise, Marcie moved out in front of her. She took a swipe at the puck but, misjudging the wet conditions, leant too far forward, causing herself to skid in the mud. She slid for some distance, turning round to face the opposite direction, while the stick was wrenched from her hands with the sheer force of the fall. The stick flew through the air. Natasha grabbed Olivia.

"Quick, Olivia, down!" she shouted as both girls lay close to the earth waiting for the sickening thud.

The stick landed just beside Natasha's right foot, narrowly missing hitting either of the girls, on almost the exact spot where Olivia had been standing a few short seconds before. Miss Starrs was running down the field, wet hair standing on end, eyes wide with horror, unsure whether or not anyone had been hurt.

"Natasha, Olivia, are you all right? Oh, thank goodness!" she said as both girls stood up. Both their faces were streaked with mud, their gym shorts and tee-shirts dirty and sodden. "Go inside and have a hot shower, girls," she said gently, "while I attend to Marcie."

Marcie too was on her feet. "I'm sorry, Olivia, Miss Starrs, I was only trying to block ..." She was crying now, her pale cheeks even paler than normal.

"Go inside, Marcie," said Miss Starrs. "On you go, follow the girls in and have a nice hot shower. I'll come and see you all in a minute or two."

Miss Starrs gently herded the girls into the

school then went back to the top of the field. She checked her watch – only about ten minutes to go. She'd let the three girls have some time to themselves and then get the rest of the class inside and cleaned up. She blew the whistle for the girls to play on, and heaved a sigh of relief. She'd thought her recently completed first aid course was going to come into its own that time! She looked around to see where Ellis had gone; Miss Starrs knew she hadn't meant any harm, but since she was the one who hit the offending shot, she was sure she'd be concerned about Olivia.

She finally spotted her, standing on her own at one side of the field. Now isn't that strange. Miss Starrs shook her head. She'd thought Olivia and Ellis were friends – maybe she was wrong. She tried to shake some of the rain from her hair and ran up the pitch to make sure nothing more untoward happened!

Ellis admired her new trainers. She thought the green flash at the side matched her new headband really well.

Marcie was towelling herself dry after her warm shower. The girl was shaking from the shock of what had almost happened.

"I really am sorry, Olivia," she kept repeating. "I was only trying to block the shot. I could see from where I was standing that Ellis was going to make a direct hit, I mean, I don't mean that she meant to hit you, just that I could see, that it looked as though . . . Oh, I don't know what I mean anymore. I really am so sorry," she finished.

Olivia put her arms round the, by now, tearful girl.

"Look, Marcie, I really appreciate what you did out there just now. You didn't hit me with your stick, though I don't know how you managed to miss!" She winked at Natasha. "But the truth is that no harm was done and I'm eternally grateful to you for getting me off that cold, wet pitch and into this lovely warm shower, so no more tears, eh?"

Marcie smiled. "Okay then, if you're sure you forgive me."

"And, hey," joked Natasha, "aren't you the dark horse, then? I thought you were supposed to hate hockey, yet there you were, diving in front of people, swinging sticks for all you're worth – quite the little sporting heroine, eh? Just shows what friends will do for you – lucky you, Olivia," she finished.

Marcie looked a bit apprehensive but when

she realised that Natasha was genuinely con-
gratulating her she visibly relaxed.

"Let's get dressed and get out of here," said
Olivia, "before the rest of the class arrive and
we're caught up in the stampede. And remember
we have to pick up our class photographs today
I can't wait to see how awful we look, and who
has the worst acne!"

Chapter 3

Marcie volunteered to pick up all three photographs and joined the queue outside the head's office. Ellis was two in front of her.

"Hey, Marcie, how are you doing now?" she smiled. "That was some display you put on this morning."

"I'm okay," Marcie replied. "You must have got a shock yourself when you realised the direction the puck was taking."

"Next," came the loud voice from just inside the headmaster's office.

Ellis stepped forward.

"See you later, Marcie," she said as she picked up her photograph and walked off down the corridor.

Marcie sighed. Why was she the one to feel so guilty in this whole incident when Ellis had played an obvious part and yet seemed to be shrugging the whole thing off. Maybe that was what happened when boys became interested in you – hockey fields became insignificant parts of your life and new 'stays put – even after kissing' lipstick took over. She wondered if she'd ever feel that way, but couldn't help but question whether boys would ever be interested in her – maybe she should dye her hair.

She handed the small package to Natasha.

"I've given Olivia hers," Marcie was out of breath from hurrying up the corridor. "She says she'll see you in class – I've got double geography, so I'll catch up with you later."

"Thanks, Marcie, see you." Natasha stuffed the photograph in her rucksack – she'd have more time to look at it later. She took her place in Mr Jenkins' French class, as usual sitting somewhere near Olivia. She liked French, and even more so since Mr Jenkins was more than a little good looking. She could listen to his almost perfect accent and look at his ruggedly handsome face for two periods every day, and not fall asleep once! She smiled briefly at Olivia before opening her text book.

Just before four o'clock, Natasha realised she'd forgotten to pick up the dry cleaning her mum had asked her to pick up when she was half asleep this morning. She'd have to run into town if she was to make it before the shop shut. She hoped Olivia remembered they had plans for this evening – she'd pass her a note, just in case. The bell rang and Natasha jumped up straight away. She pressed the note into Olivia's hand.

"Got to run," she said, "see you later."

Olivia clasped the note as she tried not to drop her books, pens, rucksack and watched Natasha almost run from the classroom.

"Where is she going in such a rush?" she wondered. "Find out tonight, I suppose."

"Did you pick up the dry cleaning?" her mum shouted, as the front door slammed.

"Yes, Mum, I remembered," she shouted

back, breathing a sigh of relief that her memory hadn't failed her!

She gave Tommy's sleeping face a quick kiss as she passed his room – he took so much out of himself he still needed a short afternoon nap – and went into her own room to change out of her dreaded uniform. Jogging bottoms and tee-shirt donned, she flopped onto her bed, hands behind her head.

"Suppose I'd better check if I have any homework now, as I probably won't get round to doing it later," she thought, picking up her rucksack.

As she rummaged around in the bag, the forgotten class photograph came to hand.

"Oh, the class photo," she smiled. "This should be good for a laugh, if previous years are anything to go by," she thought.

She tore off the cellophane paper and searched the sea of faces for her own. There she was, hair pushed untidily behind her ears, little wisps escaping from either side. She could never get it to look even remotely tidy, apart from the year her mum had taken her to the hairdressers to have it put up for a school dance she was going to. The girl at the hairdressers had taken such care over it, but even she had a hard time getting it under control. There had been so much hairspray on it, though, that Natasha decided she preferred it to look unruly rather than stuck together on top of her head!

But look, there were Ellis and Olivia standing together, and Marcie in the row in front. She was smaller than the others, so the photographer had suggested it would be better for her to be nearer the front of the class. Marcie said later she should have worn her new platform shoes, then she wouldn't have had to be split from her friends, and Paul had laughed and said it didn't matter where you stood in a photograph, you could still be the greatest of friends after the camera had flashed! Ellis had smiled at this too, though not as widely as she had smiled for the cameraman. She was so photogenic; just look at the way she played to the camera.

Natasha's eyes scanned the rest of the photograph quickly. Her eyes came to rest on the right hand side of the back row. A small, fair girl stood slightly apart from the others, her eyes not looking into the camera at all.

"Who on earth is that?" thought Natasha.

She'd never seen the girl before. Was it someone from another class who'd been put with theirs at the last minute? She didn't remember anyone being brought in, or possibly it was someone new at school altogether, but no, new starts always caused such a lot of interest, she couldn't possibly have missed out on that happening. Who was she? Olivia would surely know – she looked at her watch – only five-thirty. Olivia was due to come over about seven that night, they were going to discuss their costumes for the Halloween Ball on Friday night. Natasha wanted to go as Cleopatra, the Queen of the Nile, and her mum had promised to help make her wig. It would also be a good excuse to paint lots of make-up on, and wear jewellery half way up her arms! She propped the photograph against her CD player and went downstairs to see what was for tea.

Chapter 4

Olivia looked again at the note.

"See you at seven at the cemetery – look for Suzanna Craigson's stone."

Olivia was utterly puzzled by the note – she thought tonight was for discussing costumes – not an eerie night at the graveyard! It was so unlike Natasha, too, she wasn't exactly brave when it came to anything to do with graves and old churchyards, and especially not at seven o'clock at night just when it was beginning to get dark. She sighed and stuffed the note into her jacket pocket. After she'd helped Mum clear the dinner dishes she'd get changed and go and meet her friend, no doubt all would be revealed once she'd met up with Natasha.

Five minutes past seven. Natasha was late. Olivia had found the tombstone fairly easily as it was positioned near the front of the graveyard and could be seen quite clearly from the road. Olivia was grateful she'd worn her heavy jacket as it was beginning to get quite cold. She pulled up her collar and dug her hands deeper into her pockets.

Ten past seven.

"Olivia," she heard from behind her. She turned and saw a figure come from the direction of the cemetery gate.

"Hurry up, Natasha," she said. "Whatever were you doing in there?"

It was at that split second, she told Natasha afterwards, that she realised "Natasha" wasn't in fact Natasha at all. The person coming towards her was smaller and slighter than her friend, and she walked with a pronounced limp. Olivia tried to see the girl more clearly, but dusk had just started to fall and she couldn't quite make out her features just yet. As she approached, slowly, hindered by the limp, Olivia was able to see that the girl had long, almost golden, hair, curled in ringlets which framed her face and cascaded down her back, and she appeared to be in some distress.

"Are you okay?" Olivia ventured.

The last thing she felt like doing was standing there offering help; for some reason the approaching girl frightened her. Olivia gave herself a shake.

"Don't be so stupid," she thought, "it's merely the fact that you're right beside a cemetery, it's getting dark and the trees are casting dark shadows."

This little talking to only served to make her feel worse, though, and she found herself willing Natasha to hurry up. A bit of moral support wouldn't go wrong!

The girl had stopped now, almost directly opposite Olivia, and Olivia was aware of the strange clothes the girl was wearing. Her dress was long and frilled at the cuffs and she wore a little matching bonnet over her fair curls. She wore a funny sort of built up shoe on her right foot, and this was the leg which had seemed to drag behind her as she walked.

The girl looked directly at Olivia and Olivia noticed for the first time there was an almost ethereal quality about her. Her skin was so pale as to be almost translucent and her eyes seemed to be wet with tears.

"Are you Olivia Goulden?" she almost whispered. "I must find her, please help me. She is in great danger, I must warn her!"

She reached out her hand as though to clasp Olivia's but no touch was made. Instead, the girl's hand seemed to go right through Olivia's, bringing with it the sensation of a cold, cold wind which chilled her very soul.

Olivia was by now quite literally frozen to the spot with fear. She was so cold her teeth had begun to chatter and all she could think of was getting out of there.

"Please, you must listen to me," the girl said again. It was at this point that Olivia was unfrozen. She turned from the pale haired girl, took to her heels and ran as she had never run before. All the way along the pavement she ran, stumbling sometimes over broken paving slabs, until at last she could see Natasha's house, warm and welcoming in the distance.

She didn't even knock on the door, just burst in and ran straight upstairs to Natasha's bedroom, pushing Natasha aside as she jumped up to see what the commotion was.

"Olivia, what on earth . . . ?"

Olivia was standing to one side of the window, and had pulled back the curtain.

"Put out the light," she instructed Natasha.

"Not until you tell me what's happening," Natasha replied from the bed where she had fallen.

"Put out the damn light!" Olivia almost screamed "or I'll do it myself."

"All right, all right," answered Natasha as she jumped up to put off the switch. "Keep your voice down, you'll wake Tommy." She joined Olivia at the bedroom window to look outside, although she had no idea what she was supposed to be looking for.

"Look, there she is!" Olivia was almost hysterical. Natasha looked out of the window to see Marcie approaching the house.

"It's Marcie," said Natasha. "She rang just after six o'clock tonight to ask if she could come over and help with either of our costumes. What's the problem with that?" It was then that she noticed that Olivia's hands, and practically her whole body, were shaking.

"Olivia, you have to calm down and tell me

what happened out there – I have no idea what's going on. Come on, come and sit on the bed with me."

Olivia allowed herself to be led to the bed where she promptly sat down and burst into tears. Marcie had arrived, and knocked on the front door. Tommy woke up and started to cry. Mrs Morris answered the door and brought Marcie in.

"Do me a favour, pet," she said, "go and start heating some milk for Tommy – he likes a hot milky drink if he wakes at this time – and I'll go and bring him downstairs."

"Sure, Mrs Morris," agreed Marcie. She just adored chubby little Tommy and didn't mind helping out with him before she joined her friends upstairs.

Olivia, meanwhile, had just recounted her story to her friend.

"But what on earth were you doing standing about at the cemetery?" asked Natasha.

Olivia turned, aghast, to Natasha. "Because you told me to meet you there, in your note," she replied.

"In my note. What note? The one I passed you in French?"

"Oh no, not again," thought Natasha. Was she going mad? "Let me see the note, Olivia, please. I know I didn't ask to meet you at the cemetery, I just know I didn't, let me see the note, please."

Olivia took the now tattered note from her jacket pocket and handed it to her friend. Sure enough, the note said what Olivia had said it did, except that, for Natasha, it was even more frightening.

"See you at seven at the cemetery – look for

Suzanna Craigson's stone." Suzanna Craigson! The grave Natasha had noticed for the first time the other day.

Natasha shook her head in disbelief.

"I have no idea what on earth is going on here, Olivia, I swear it. I did not write 'at the cemetery' on that note, I merely wrote 'See you at seven'. I mean, you know how I feel about graves and things, there's just no way I would have asked you to hang around there waiting for me." She sighed deeply. "I don't know what to do here, Olivia, you do believe me don't you?" She looked at her friend.

Olivia lifted tear-stained eyes.

"Yes, Natasha, but only because it's you and I've known you too long to think you would ever deliberately frighten me. But it still doesn't solve the puzzle. What on earth is happening here? First, my full name was written on the initial note, then words are seemingly added to the second note and then that, that *person* outside just now . . ." Olivia started to shake again.

"We'd better get ourselves together before Marcie joins us – we don't want to frighten her half to death with some half-baked story about notes and ghostly apparitions," said Natasha.

"Half-baked story?" protested Olivia.

"Yes, I know what you saw, and I believe you," said Natasha "but will anybody else? Honestly, we should keep this whole thing under wraps until we know exactly what's going on."

"So, what's Ellis coming to the party as?" asked Marcie as she deftly glued some more sequins on Olivia's dress. Olivia had decided to go as a gangster's moll – she was a real old movie buff and had just finished watching a season of gang-ster movies where all the molls wore sequinned dresses, fur stoles, and lashings of glossy red lip-stick!

"Don't know – she hasn't mentioned it at all," replied Olivia.

"Don't suppose for a minute it'll be any-thing unglamorous, though. Can't imagine Ellis doing anything remotely unglamorous, can you?" Natasha smiled. "Well, we're not exactly dressing down for the event, are we girls?"

She looked at Marcie. "What are you com-ing as, Marcie. Hey, listen, if you don't have a costume yet why don't you come as Al Capone, you know, the infamous Chicago gangster, then you could partner Olivia. You could borrow my dad's braces, and I'm sure we could get a violin case from someone, you know, to pretend it was a machine gun – Marcie, are you listening to a word I'm saying?"

She turned to the other girl who still sat, head bowed, gluing sequins on Olivia's dress.

"Yes, Natasha, I hear you," she replied. "And thanks. It's just that my mum said she would find a costume for me – something about family tradition." Marcie lowered her head again and returned to the task in hand.

Natasha and Olivia exchanged glances but said nothing. Sometimes they wondered about Marcie's family. She seemed to have a very strict upbringing – perhaps because she was an only child they supposed. Better to say nothing, anyway.

Olivia threw a rolled up leather belt in Natasha's direction. "Made you this, Natasha, it's an asp, remember, Cleopatra needs a snake."

Natasha screamed loudly. "Get that away from me, Olivia, there's no way I'm putting an asp near me – Cleopatra or not!"

Natasha's room door was pushed open to reveal Mrs Morris standing in the hallway.

"If you girls wake Tommy again you won't be going to the Halloween Ball," she threatened. "Now keep it down, please."

Chapter 5

Next day at school, Natasha, Olivia and Ellis stood chatting in the playground.

"Still seeing Scott, then Ellis?" Olivia asked.

"Yes, we went to the cinema last night – saw a really scary film, you know the one about the Zombies in the shopping mall?"

"Zombies? – are you mad?" laughed Natasha. "I thought young lovers were supposed to go see romantic movies and sit in the back row?"

Ellis laughed too. "I know, I don't actually think Scott and I are romantically suited – I'd rather sit and watch a good scary film than snog in the back row. Olivia, is something wrong?"

Olivia had turned from the two girls and was staring at Marcie who was walking slowly towards them. Except that she wasn't walking – she was limping and dragging her leg behind her.

"Wh—what have you done to your leg?" she stammered.

Marcie drew alongside the girls.

"I fell over when I came out of the shower last night – the floor was a bit wet and I slid," she finished. "I have to go," she said, "I've got social studies first period and you know what Mr Livingstone's like for timekeeping."

"Bye, Marcie," the girls shouted as they watched her disappear up the steep stone stairs and through the front doors of the high school.

"I have to run, too," said Ellis. "See you at lunchtime."

"Bye, Ellis," said Natasha. "Olivia, are you all right?" she asked her friend. Olivia gave herself a shake.

"Yes, I'm okay, Natasha. It's just that with the colour of Marcie's hair, and then the limp, she looked just like . . ."

"It's okay, Olivia, I know who you mean. Suzanna Craigson's uppermost in my mind too, though I'm trying hard not to think about her."

Just at that moment the bell rang summoning the girls to that morning's classes.

"Let's go," Natasha took her friend's arm. "We can talk more about this at morning break."

Break was a long time coming. Natasha spent the whole of the first two periods decorating the front of her book with drawings of eyes. Cleopatra's eyes with thick black liner and gold lashes, Cleopatra's eyes with thick green liner and blue lashes, Cleopatra's eyes with thick silver liner and gold lashes! She was just debating whether or not to paint her nails two different colours when she was startled by the bell ringing. She stuffed her books into her schoolbag and, as she did so, came across the class photograph she had put into her bag the previous evening so that she could ask Olivia who the mystery girl was.

She joined Olivia in the queue for the tuck shop.

"Wait till I show you this!" Natasha took the class photograph from inside her bag and showed it to Olivia. "Notice anything strange?" she asked her friend.

Olivia scanned the photograph.

"Oh my God, it's her!" she stammered, "Natasha, that's her, the girl at the graveyard, the one at the top right of the photograph." She turned to Natasha, "I don't understand – just what's going on here?"

People were turning round to stare.

"Shh, Olivia," Natasha again took her friend's arm and guided her away from the queue towards the quietness of the cloak room.

"What on earth do you mean, it's her? I can't believe what I'm hearing," said Natasha. "Do you mean the girl in the photograph is Suzanna Craigson?"

Olivia was no longer listening instead she was rummaging inside her own schoolbag.

"Here it is," she said triumphantly as she pulled out her own copy of the class picture. She pulled the cellophane from the print and thrust it in front of Natasha's eyes.

"Look," she cried, "she's not in my photograph, there's nothing weird about mine, who's been tampering with yours? None of this is making any sense. Who would want to paint a face into your photograph? Who is this Suzanna Craigson?" She started to cry.

Natasha took Olivia's photograph and looked at it long and hard. Sure enough, the girls in the back row of this photograph were all classmates and well known to them and there was no sign of the slight, fair haired girl who stood at the top right hand corner on her own.

"I don't know the answers to any of your questions, Olivia, but I want to find out just as much as you do. Whoever Suzanna Craigson is, we're going to find out, and find out soon.

Come on, don't cry any more, it's all right now."

Olivia wiped at her eyes with the sleeve of her jacket. Natasha held both the photographs in her hands. She must try and stay calm, for Olivia's sake, as well as her own. She turned the photographs over and saw that Olivia's name was written on Natasha's copy, and vice versa. Marcie must have mixed up the prints when she picked them up the previous day.

"Olivia, it looks as if you've had my copy," she said. "Look, your name's on mine," and she showed the backs of both photographs to the girl. "Not that it matters one little bit," she finished.

"Oh, but it does," Olivia rejoined. "Don't you see, Suzanna said she had to talk to me, that I was in great danger. She seems to be trying to contact me somehow, adding things to your notes, appearing outside the cemetery, and now this, appearing in my picture! I don't know if I can take much more of this." Olivia was ashen white.

Natasha tried to appear reassuring.

"Come on," she said purposefully, "we have two more classes this morning then at lunchtime, you and I, my friend, are going to the library."

"We're meeting Ellis, and probably Marcie, at lunchtime, though Natasha."

"Blast," said Natasha, "well, we'll just have to wait until four o'clock then. No more notes," she smiled, "we'll make our plans face to face from now on!"

"Why are we going there anyway?" asked Olivia, puzzled.

"Because they keep old newspapers, things of interest which have happened in town for the last hundred years or so, and if there's anything of any interest there to do with Suzanna Craigson we're going to find it."

Olivia shuddered. Thank goodness Natasha was so brave and sensible, or at least pretending to be, because Olivia wasn't coping with this thing very well at all. Natasha replaced the two photographs inside her school bag as both girls made their way to their next class. Neither she nor Olivia noticed that the girl at the top right corner of Olivia's class photograph had completely faded out of sight.

Mrs Florence looked at both girls over the rim of her glasses.

"Not usual to see you two young ladies in the library after school," she stated.

Natasha sighed. "I know, Mrs Florence, but we've decided to take part in a new project – life back in the 1900s right here in our own little town, and we thought you'd be the best person to help us out. Not that I'm insinuating that you're old, or anything," she continued, "just that maybe you could point us in the right direction for any news cuttings, history books, old pictures, etc, that could help us out – you know the kind of thing I mean."

The seemingly frosty, but kind-hearted librarian almost smiled.

"This way then, girls," she led them towards the narrow winding staircase of the old library, "and hurry, before any other potential knowledge seekers come in looking for assistance."

The girls had never been upstairs in the library before. Indeed, it wasn't one of their most favoured haunts at all. They could always find much more exciting things to do outwith school hours, or at least up until now they had!

"When you reach the top, the books on your left will help with the history of the actual town of Chalmersville, then the shelves below have hanging files which should contain old newspapers – in chronological order, which I don't want messed up!" she added before returning to the main desk. "If you need any help, you'll have to come down, I really can't leave the desk unmanned in case it get busy."

Her words faded into the distance as the two girls climbed higher and higher up into the top part of the old library.

Natasha and Olivia exchanged glances.

"Busy?" Natasha raised her eyebrows.

"When was the last time you saw a queue form outside the library?"

Olivia giggled. "Shh, she'll hear you, and we may need her help later, you never know."

"She won't hear us," replied Natasha, "listen, can't you hear her – 'stamp, stamp', she just loves putting that 'overdue' stamp on the returned books."

The girls had by now reached their destination.

"Gosh, what a musty smell," said Olivia as she plonked herself down on the dusty floor.

"It'll get even worse by the time we've finished," returned Natasha. "Just look at how thick the dust is on top of this book."

She pulled a large brown book from one of the top shelves and opened it on the top of the desk in front of her.

"Okay, Olivia, you start on the newspapers. Now let's see, if I remember correctly Suzanna lived from November 1906 to October 1920, so see if you can find anything about her from the papers. Here," she drew two bags of crisps from inside her jacket pocket, "sustenance."

Two hours later, the girls had made little progress. The name Craigson, Natasha had discovered, was relatively new to Chalmersville. New, being a couple of hundred years old, that is. The family had settled there in a house, the description of which meant nothing to either of the girls. They decided that the house must no longer exist or, if it did, it had been changed so much by the present owner that it bore no resemblance to the description in the book.

"Wait a minute," said Olivia excitedly. "Look at this!"

Tragedy within Craigson Household. A young girl was today recovered from the boating pond outside her home at Gatefells after a fatal drowning incident.

Natasha slammed her book shut and gave her full attention to what Olivia was reading.

"That's where Ellis lives, Gatefells, go on Olivia, don't stop there."

Mr and Mrs Craigson, who today lost their only child, are understandably distraught and have asked that they be left alone with their grief.

There the story stopped, though in a later article the girls were able to read more about the family. Apparently not much was known of the couple, being relative newcomers to Chalmersville, although Mr Craigson was fast becoming a well known figure in the community through his tireless work helping charitable organisations. They found that the girl who had drowned had, indeed, been named Suzanna. She had gone out on her own in the boat, despite having been warned by her parents on previous occasions that she should always be accompanied. If she had been accompanied by someone, there was no evidence of this. The article also said that she was of poor health and wore a built up shoe as she had been born with one leg shorter than the other. Olivia gave a sharp intake of breath.

"It's just got to have been the same person, Natasha, the girl in the photograph and at the graveside. But why is she trying to reach me now? Oh, I wish I understood what was going on. It's not so long ago I didn't even believe in ghosts!"

Natasha continued to flick through several newspapers.

"At least we've found out some information, Olivia, the day's not been completely wasted. I mean, we now know that Suzanna Craigson did live in a house in Chalmersville, that she was killed in a boating accident and that she was an only child." She stopped.

"So what, Natasha? I mean, I'm sorry, but how exactly does that help us to discover why on earth she wants to get in touch with me?" Olivia sighed.

"Patience, my dear, we'll get to the bottom of this little mystery soon enough," Natasha replied. "And, hey, did you work out those dates? 2 November to 1 November 1920 – that means she died the day before her birthday, the day after Halloween. That's just got to have some significance. It's too creepy not to. Come on, let's get out of here, before we get put back up on the shelves with the rest of the old relics here! I feel so dusty I can't wait to get home and have a shower."

The two girls climbed back down the winding staircase, dusting themselves down as they went.

"Thanks, Mrs Florence," they shouted to the librarian.

"Shh, girlies," she held her finger to her lips.

"Sorry," they giggled, "didn't think there was anyone here to disturb," as indeed there wasn't. Luckily for them, Mrs Florence didn't hear their last remark.

She followed them to the door.

"I hope you put everything back in chronological order," she bent over to speak to the two girls. "I put in a lot of hard work organising those papers, you know," she finished.

"Yes, of course we did," smiled Natasha, "and thank you for all your help, Mrs Florence, we might need to come back another day, and it's great to know you'll be here for us to rely on," she gushed.

Mrs Florence pushed a loose tendril of hair back behind her glasses.

"Always a pleasure to see you both," she flushed. "Any time, girls." She closed the door gently behind them both.

"Natasha?" said Olivia as they crossed the road outside the library to begin the journey home.

"Yes?" said Natasha absent-mindedly.

"What's chronological?"

Chapter 6

Olivia was excited about the Halloween Ball to-night and felt as though her geography lesson would never end. She and Natasha both had their costumes ready and couldn't wait to get home and dressed up.

"I wonder what Marcie and Ellis are doing? Maybe they told Natasha and she forgot to say, or maybe it's a big secret," Olivia mused.

Both she and Natasha had made a pact to forget all about Suzanna Craigson for this one night and simply go to the Halloween Ball and have just that – a ball! The bell began to ring and, as one, the pupils threw books, pens and anything else that came to hand into their bags. Olivia caught up with Natasha outside the class.

"Thought that was never going to end!" she smiled at her friend.

Natasha smiled back. "Hey, Ellis," she called.

Olivia looked in the direction Natasha was facing and saw Ellis' retreating back as she left the school building. Her dark curls bobbed as she flounced out of the door but she seemed not to hear her friend's shout as she carried on walking.

"Strange," said Natasha, "I could have sworn she saw us, and I'm almost positive she's not far enough away that she wouldn't have heard me shout." She looked puzzled for a second or two. "Ah well, never mind, let's get out of here. We've got a lot to do before we meet up tonight, and then we'll discover the secrets behind Marcie's and Ellis's costumes!"

The school hall was brightly lit, not just by lights but by strategically placed pumpkins with the insides removed to make room for short, dumpy candles. One by one the pupils arrived, exclaiming over the others' costumes, guessing the identity of those who wore masks. Loud music filled the hall from the disco set up on the stage and banners suspended from the ceiling carried the words "Welcome to the 1997 Chalmersville Halloween Ball". Natasha was just arriving and was trying to adjust her wig as she got out of her mother's car.

"For Heaven's sake, Natasha, leave it alone, will you, or you'll end up with no wig on at all!" her mother sighed.

"Bye, Cleo," Tommy smiled from the back seat, his little fingers opening and closing over his chubby little hand as he waved her goodbye. He couldn't quite get his tongue round Cleopatra so Natasha had said Cleo would do very nicely.

"Goodbye, sweetheart," she blew a kiss as she stepped out onto the street.

"Now, Natasha," her mother began.

"I know, Mum," she interrupted, "I won't be late." Mrs Morris smiled as she put the car into gear and made to draw away from the kerb.

"Have a nice time, Natasha, goodbye."

Natasha waved at Tommy as he waved out of the back window then, with one last pull at her wig, she joined the other party-goers as they entered the hall.

"Over here, Natasha," she heard Olivia call.

She turned to see her friend, cigarette holder in silken gloved hand, wearing her beaded, sequinned dress and topped by a small hat with a very large feather.

"Olivia, you look terrific," she laughed as she joined her friend.

"So do you, Nat, your make-up's fantastic. You look like a dead person reincarnated, your eyes are so black!"

The two girls laughed together and went in search of the rest of their classmates. There was to be a prize for the best costume and most of the pupils had made a bit of an effort to get in the running. A passing gorilla growled at Olivia. Olivia laughed.

"Unfortunately I'll never know who he is. There are at least six different gorillas here."

The girls made their way towards the end of the hall where soft drinks were being served.

"Hey, look, there's Batman over there," smiled Natasha, "and Catwoman's with him. Just look at the length of her claws, and I thought my false nails were long!"

A rather fat Indian squaw stood at the side of the soft drinks table, smiling now and again at a sequinned Elvis.

"Isn't this just the best fun?" Natasha nudged Olivia. "Olivia – what on earth's wrong with you?"

Olivia looked to be in some sort of trance, but the look of fear on her face told Natasha there was something very wrong. She followed Olivia's gaze to the far side of the hall they had just left and saw immediately what had caught her friend's attention. A slight, fair haired girl had just entered the room. She wore a long, cream coloured gown which was very old fashioned and, had frills round the cuffs and hem. On the back of her head she wore a small matching bonnet.

"Oh my God!" Natasha breathed. "It can't be – can it?" The two girls stood as though they were rooted to the spot. Then Natasha felt a tug on her arm.

"Hi, girls."

Natasha turned round.

"It's me, Marcie."

She was dressed in a pale blue dress with a short white apron tied around it. In her hair she wore a large Alice band and under her arm she had tucked a white rabbit. Natasha tried to regain her composure. She had hoped that the girl they had been looking at in the distance was in fact Marcie, but if the girl standing beside her was Marcie dressed as Alice in Wonderland then that ruled that possibility out!

"Hi, Marcie," she said. "Olivia," she pulled on her friend's arm. "Look, isn't Marcie a brilliant Alice."

Olivia turned. "Oh, yes, yes," stumbled Olivia. "Your costume's just great."

She tried to show some enthusiasm, but kept feeling her eyes being dragged back to the slight figure at the other end of the room.

"Told you – family tradition," Marcie continued. "Apparently my great, great, great aunt, or someone, actually I'm not sure how many greats it is, knew Lewis Carroll, you know the person who wrote *Alice in Wonderland* and

Through the Looking Glass and based Alice's sister on her character. I mean I know she only played a small part, the sister, that is, but our family became very Alice-orientated after that. Every Halloween we use it as an opportunity to indulge a little in the book's characters. I've gone as a white rabbit before, though that can get very hot and stuffy . . ."

Marcie's voice droned on and on in the background and by this time Natasha was paying her as little attention as Olivia had been.

"Marcie, I hate to be rude, but there's someone we must see at the end of the room. We'll be back in a minute or two – excuse us."

The two girls moved away and hurried to the far end of the room. Marcie turned away, feeling slightly miffed, and limped towards the drinks' table. As Natasha and Olivia approached, the fair haired girl turned towards them with a smile on her lips.

"Hello, Natasha, Olivia," she murmured. "What do you think, then?"

Natasha and Olivia stopped in their tracks. Olivia looked quizzically at the girl.

"Ellis?" she questioned.

"Blast!" said Ellis. "I knew you'd guess it was me – it's the dark eyebrows, isn't it?" Natasha and Olivia started to breathe again. Natasha's eyes travelled to Ellis' feet, but she wore normal shoes, not a built up one like the real Suzanna.

"But who are you supposed to be?" the girls asked.

"Well, I know I'm not anyone famous, really," said Ellis, "but Mum found a trunk in the attic and this was one of the outfits inside. It was just such a good fit, and I haven't had time to make anything, what with seeing Scott and everything, so I decided I'd just come looking as a young Chalmersville girl would look about 100 years ago! You two look very glamorous though, maybe I made the wrong choice," finished Ellis.

"No, you look really great," Natasha managed. "Listen, we left Marcie by the drinks', we'll have to go back and get her – are you coming?"

"Yes, in a minute or two, I just want to find Scott. He said he was dressing as a gorilla – I don't suppose you've seen him, have you?"

Olivia and Natasha rejoined Marcie.

"Marcie, I'm really sorry," said Olivia. "Let me have a proper look at your costume."

Marcie smiled.

"Well I have to admit I was a bit hurt earlier, but I'll forgive you both," she twirled, showing the full flounces of the skirt, with the stiff net petticoat underneath. "Don't know how they ever wore these things though," she said "give me a pair of good old jogging bottoms any day!"

The girls laughed. Natasha and Olivia smiled at one another.

"Come on," said Olivia as they went on to the dance floor, "let's have what we said we were going to have – a ball!"

All too soon, as is wont to happen when you are enjoying yourself, the evening was over. The pumpkins had lost their glow, as had most of the guests, and parents' cars were drawing up outside to pick up their children. The four friends stood on the top step outside the school hall.

"Oh, I almost forgot," said Ellis. "Mum said I could invite you three over tomorrow, seeing it's Saturday, for some lunch. Pleeee-ease say you'll come. She and Dad are going out for the day and the house will be ours to do what we want. Come on, girls, you've never been to mine before, say you can make it."

The girls looked pleased at the invitation, Ellis was right, they hadn't been to her house before.

"We'll be there," they returned.

"Great," smiled Ellis, "be there for twelve o'clock – you too, Alice," she nudged Marcie. "And bring your white rabbit if you like!" Ellis ran off down the steps.

"Wait, Ellis, don't you want a lift?" shouted Olivia.

But Ellis was gone, fair ringlets streaming behind her as she ran off into the darkness.

"Ah well, seems like she didn't want a lift,"

Olivia finished as her father's car pulled up at the kerb side.

The three girls clambered in, stifling yawns as they pulled on seat belts and yanked at annoying wigs, stiff petticoats and tutted at sequinless patches of dress.

"Not turned into pumpkins yet, then?" joked Mr Goulden.

"No, Dad," returned Olivia, "nor did any of us meet our handsome princes."

Natasha leaned her head back against her seat and closed her eyes for the short car journey in front of her.

Chapter 7

"Monkey nuts? You can't be serious, Natasha, you want to take monkey nuts with you?" Olivia couldn't believe she was hearing her friend.

"It's just for fun," Natasha laughed down the phone. "I mean it is the day after Halloween – maybe Ellis was planning on having us bobbing for apples – you never know. Anyway, my mum bought in loads of nuts and she still has them in the kitchen. I'll fill a few bags and bring them."

Olivia had gone rather quiet on the other end of the phone.

"Are you still there, Olivia?" Natasha asked.

"Yes, I'm still here, Natasha. It was just with you saying this was the day after Hallow-een and I remembered the date. November the first. It was on this day in 1920 that Suzanna died – remember?" Natasha had momentarily forgotten.

"Yes, I do remember, Olivia. Look, shall we do what we did last night? Go to Ellis' house, have a good time and put Suzanna to the back of our minds for now? I mean, let's face it, nothing strange has happened for a couple of days – maybe the whole thing was in our imagination."

Olivia started to protest.

"No, okay, I know you're right, we couldn't

have imagined the things that happened. Let's say then that after today we look at this whole thing again, go back to the library, maybe ask Mrs Florence some direct questions. You never know what she might be able to help us with."

Olivia took a deep breath.

"Okay, Natasha, I guess you're right. I'll meet you at the bottom of the lane next to the new Health Centre – I'll give Marcie a call and tell her we'll wait for her there, too. See you in half an hour or so."

Olivia hung up the phone. Natasha was right. She must put this thing to the back of her mind. Suzanna Craigson was dead, and there was absolutely nothing she, Olivia Goulden, could do about that. She picked up the phone and dialled Marcie's number.

There was no reply from Marcie's home.

"Strange," thought Olivia, "maybe she's already gone up to Ellis's house, though I'd have thought she would have wanted to meet up with Natasha and me and all go up together. Maybe she's gone to the shops to pick up some things before she goes and we'll meet her en route."

Olivia ran up stairs to pick up her warm jacket. It could be quite chilly outside these days, and she wasn't sure if Ellis planned for them to spend the day indoors or out. Better to be prepared.

"Come on, slowcoach," shouted Natasha. "It's freezing standing about here."

Olivia hurried along the pavement towards her friend.

"Sorry, I kept trying Marcie's number before I came out, but I can't get a hold of her," replied Olivia.

Natasha shrugged.

"She's maybe already at Ellis's house – who knows? Let's hurry up, anyway, hopefully she'll have something hot to drink waiting for us."

The girls began their ascent towards Gatefells, for the house was situated almost at the highest point of the town, and they climbed together in companionable silence – the silence that comes only from knowing someone your whole life.

Olivia broke the silence to ask, "Do you know what Ellis's father does for a living, Natasha? The family certainly seem to be very well off."

Again, Natasha shrugged.

"No, I kept meaning to ask my mum, but I

never did. All I know is they live in a large, posh house on the top of this hill and that Ellis never wants for anything!"

The girls were now in the grounds of the old house and Natasha was struck not only by the beauty of the large gardens which surrounded the house, but by the sheer size of everything.

"Wouldn't it just be a dream to live here, Olivia? Look at the grand scale of everything."

Olivia didn't answer. Since she had entered the grounds of the house, she had been feeling ever so slightly on edge.

"Didn't there used to be gates here?" she asked Natasha, pointing to the edge of the lawn. Natasha turned to look at her.

"Now, how would I know that, Olivia? I've only passed in this direction once or twice before, and both of those times I was in the car. As far as I know there weren't any gates."

"Then, how is it that I remember large wrought iron gates, supported on either side by stone pillars?" asked Olivia. "And I know that that oak tree over there used to hold a swing in the summertime"

Olivia was becoming more and more animated now as she spoke. Her eyes were bright as she looked all around her.

"There, look, the window I used to sit at while Ellen prepared dinner. If you sat in a certain position just before dusk fell you could see Papa dismount . . ."

Natasha was staring very hard at Olivia. This whole thing had affected her friend more than she could have imagined. Natasha took both Olivia's hands in her own.

"Olivia, you have to calm down! Olivia, please!"

Olivia's eyes were wild, darting in every direction. She was smiling, laughing almost, but it was a hollow laughter which chilled Natasha's very heart.

"Olivia, please, you're frightening me. Who is Ellen? Papa dismounting? I don't know what you're talking about."

"Natasha, Olivia, over here," both girls turned. Ellis was standing in the doorway to the house, waving frantically. "Come on, you two," she shouted "I thought you'd never get here."

Natasha turned back towards Olivia, still holding both her hands. The wild eyed look had gone, and her own Olivia again stood beside her.

"I'm, I'm all right, Natasha, honestly, I don't know what happened just then. I had the strangest feeling that . . . oh, never mind, come on," she rubbed at her eyes as though she had just woken from a deep sleep and pulled the collar of her jacket up even further. "Ellis is waiting for us, let's go."

Both girls walked up the short path which led to the front entrance of Gatefells, each of them trying to put aside their uneasy thoughts.

Ellis led them into the enormous kitchen. There was a blazing log fire in the large fireplace and she had just boiled the kettle.

"Okay, chocolate and peppermint, chocolate and orange, chocolate and coconut, chocolate and chocolate?" she held up the little sachets of drinking chocolate one at a time.

"Oh, anything, so long as it's warm," smiled Natasha. "It's really cold out there today."

Ellis turned to pour the boiling liquid into the waiting mugs and Natasha stole a glance at Olivia. She seemed to be completely back to normal. She took the hot mug from Ellis gratefully and cupped both hands around it.

"Thanks, Ellis. Is Marcie not here, then?" she enquired.

"Haven't seen her yet," Ellis joined the girls at the oak table. "I thought you were all coming together."

"Well, yes," said Olivia, "that was the plan, but I couldn't reach her on the telephone and assumed she'd come up earlier on her own. Never mind, maybe we can phone her again in a while?"

Ellis nodded.

"Sure, why not. Listen, if you've started to heat up, give me your jackets and I'll hang them up for you just now, then you'll feel the benefit of them once we go back outside."

"We're going outside?" asked Natasha. "My toes are just beginning to thaw out and you're talking about going back outside?"

"Oh, don't be such a wimp, Natasha." Ellis dug the girl playfully in the ribs as she walked past her to hang up the jackets. "It's only November, for Heaven's sake, there's a lot colder weather to come. I thought you two would love to have a bit of a forage around the grounds later, since it's your first time here."

Olivia shifted in her seat.

"I, for one, would love to have a look round, Ellis. I'm quite interested in the history of the place – perhaps you can fill us in on the details."

Ellis smiled.

"Well, Mum and Dad would probably be better at that, though I do know some things, I'll try my best."

Natasha raised her eyebrows in Olivia's direction.

"Oh well," she thought, "perhaps it's for the best to find out more about this place. After all, it seems to strike a chord of recognition with Olivia, and maybe Ellis can explain away some of the morning's weird events."

She helped herself to a chocolate biscuit and pulled her chair closer to the open fire.

Chapter 8

"Ellis, I need to use your bathroom," said Olivia.

"Okay, go back out the way we came in, take your first left then first right – you can't miss it," Ellis replied. "Meanwhile, Natasha and I will go down to the library – if you want to find out about the history of Gatefells, that's the place to do it! I'll take Natasha first, then meet you back in the kitchen."

Natasha and Ellis made their way from the

kitchen down some winding stairs that led to a long narrow corridor.

"Wow!" exclaimed Natasha, "are these your ancestors?" She looked at the rows of paintings that lined the corridor.

"Yes, some of them are," Ellis replied, "that's great uncle Nicholas, and that's his wife in the small painting above his own. Don't think they had any children. Okay, not far now."

The passageway was getting darker and darker the further the girls travelled. Suddenly Ellis stopped in front of a door. She tried to turn the handle.

"It's a bit stiff, I'm afraid – not used very much these days." She gave it a hefty push and the door slowly opened.

"Where's the light?" asked Natasha as she peered into the darkness. To her utter surprise and amazement she felt a tremendous push from behind. "Ellis, what are you doing?" she almost screamed. Ellis seemed to smile in the dark passageway and gave one final push.

"Sorry, Natasha," she muttered as she bolted the door from the outside. "No hard feelings, and all that, just need to get you out of the way for now."

Natasha, plunged into blackness, had fallen down the small flight of stairs inside what appeared to be some sort of cellar.

"Ellis," she cried, "let me out of here! If this is some sort of a game . . ."

She tried to stand but had hurt her ankle in the fall. Her hand felt wet when she lifted it to brush the hair from her eyes. She must have cut it on the rough edge of the stairs when she tried to break her fall. And what was that noise?

Something scuttled past her, and she could just about make out its shape in the darkness.

"Oh God," she thought, by now terrified and hurting, "not rats, please God, not rats."

"Where's Natasha?" Olivia asked as Ellis returned to the kitchen.

"Oh, she's looking something up, she said, then she's joining us outside. Here, I brought your jacket."

"But aren't we going to the library with Natasha first?" asked Olivia.

"No, no," Ellis reassured her, "she said she'd only be a minute or two then she'd come and get us. Come on, let's go, and I'll show you around. I thought you were curious. Aren't you?"

Olivia took her jacket from Ellis's extended hand.

"Oh, yes, I'm curious all right, where shall we start?"

The two girls made their way outside and round the back of the house.

"The boating lake – it's still here!" cried Olivia.

"Yes, it's still here," returned Ellis "and why wouldn't it be?"

"Well, I just thought, you know, with Suzanna being drowned here and everything, that maybe the lake would have been drained and filled in," said Olivia.

Ellis did not register surprise at the mention of Suzanna's name

"Oh, no," replied Ellis. "These old boating lakes have their uses, you know," she smiled at Olivia. "Let's go out in the boat, it looks a bit old, I know, but it's quite safe really."

Olivia started to follow her, then stopped in her tracks.

"Ellis – do you know the story of Suzanna, then? It's just that you didn't stop me just now to ask how I knew about it."

Ellis turned to face her.

"Of course I know the story – she was a relative, you know. Come on, you first. I'll hold your hand while you step into the boat."

"I'm not very sure," Olivia started. "I mean, do your parents allow you . . ."

"Just get in, Olivia," Ellis snapped, almost pushing the girl into the boat.

"Ellis, don't push, you'll rock the boat."

Ellis laughed.

"Don't push, Ellis, you'll rock the boat," she mimicked in a childish voice. "Always the helpless little baby, aren't we, hiding behind

Natasha. Well, Miss Goulden, I've had just about enough of your whining little ways."

She began to unfasten the boat from its moorings.

"She's gone mad," thought Olivia. Where on earth was Natasha? "Ellis, please stop this," she pleaded.

"Oh no," returned Ellis, "I can't stop now – I've waited years for this, don't you see, I have to avenge Suzanna. Suzanna Craigson, you remember, the girl who died here. Except she shouldn't have died. Let me turn the clock back for you. Are you sitting comfortably? Then I'll begin."

Ellis cleared her throat, while the boat started to drift ever so slowly away from the lake's edge.

"The Craigson family – mother, father and

Suzanna, that is, settled here over 100 years ago. Suzanna was their only child, deeply loved by both. The girl was introverted, and did not make friends easily because she was self-conscious about a slight disability. But the townsfolk frowned on incomers in those days, especially those who were a little different. One day, however, a woman knocked on the door of Gatefells to enquire whether or not the Craigsons needed a housekeeper. Mrs Craigson was unsure at first, having managed so far to keep house very well on her own, but when she invited the woman in and opened the door wide, she saw the woman, too had a daughter, roughly the same age as Suzanna. There was no mention of a husband, however, and Mrs Craigson took pity on the two and engaged the woman as a housekeeper, probably thinking at the same time that the young girl would be company for her own daughter.

"Ellen, the housekeeper, worked diligently from morning till night. At first, she kept her daughter with her in the kitchen but then, finding that Suzanna would sit outside, staring into the kitchen, as though waiting for the girl, she gradually allowed Jemma to spend some time with her. The two girls soon became inseparable and the Craigson household rang with their laughter. Mr and Mrs Craigson were delighted with the way things were progressing and told Ellen, as she served up their evening meal, how it had been a fortuitous day when she came to Gatesfell. Of course, these things are never what they seem, are they?"

Ellis paused and glared at Olivia.

"Just as you're probably not what you

seem, either, Olivia, little miss goody two-shoes. Are you frightened? Wish your friend was with you?"

She gave a little laugh and pushed the boat out a little further with the paddle.

"Anyway, to get back to the matter in hand. Jemma, underneath it all, really carried a big chip on her shoulders you see. She had started off life as an illegitimate child – and it was a big deal then, you know – she felt inferior to Suzanna, and she hated having to watch her mother slave from morning to night, making sure everything was done for the Craigsons' comfort. So she hit upon a plan. Very straightforward and logical, I suppose, if you need to get rid of someone, and they happen to have a boating lake right on their doorstep, to simply take them out on the lake one day and drown them.

She planned it right down to the finest detail. She believed, you see, that if Suzanna was out of the picture then there was the possibility that Mr and Mrs Craigson would become even more attached to her, and possibly even adopt her! Though she didn't exactly want to be parted from her mother, being adopted would mean she would inherit, and she and her mother would never have to beg, borrow or steal again.

"She knew Mr and Mrs Craigson were fond of her, and she did everything in her power to wheedle her way even more into their affections. There used to be a boat house here at that time, and she put dry clothes there on the fateful day in preparation for what was to come. Mr and Mrs Craigson had gone into town to pick up the new dress they'd had made for Suzanna's birthday party. She would be fourteen years old the next day, and they were planning to take the girls to a fancy new restaurant that had just opened in the next town. Jemma had been given one of Suzanna's castoffs to wear, a perfectly good dress which fitted very well, but to Jemma it was the final straw.

" 'Today's the day, then,' she decided. As Mr and Mrs Craigson made to set off that morning, Jemma made sure they saw her dress in her outdoor clothes. 'I'm just going to visit old Mrs Lawrence,' she told them, 'Mama says she's not been very well recently, so I'll take over some of her herbal cough remedy to ease her chest a bit.' 'What a kindly girl,' they both thought as they waved goodbye.

"Great how you can just fool some people, isn't it?" said Ellis, again coming back to the present.

Olivia was as white as a sheet. Slowly, the boat was drifting steadily to the centre of the lake and Olivia could feel that her feet were wet.

"Oh, didn't I tell you?" laughed Ellis. "There's a hole in the bottom of the boat. Just a small one, mind, but big enough to let the boat fill up in about half an hour. Just long enough, I think, to make sure you're frightened half to death – then you'll know what poor Suzanna went through!"

Olivia looked down and, sure enough, there was a hole just at the far end of the boat and a small puddle had gathered there.

"Ellis, please," she begged. "I don't under-stand, really I don't. What does all this have to do with me? Why are you making me pay for Suzanna's death? I didn't have anything to do with it. I couldn't have, it was before I was born! Ellis, please help me!"

But Ellis just seemed to stare right through her. Her eyes, which Natasha had thought so beautiful, looked now to be cold as steel. Olivia knew, deep in her heart, that Ellis would never help her, she seemed to have completely lost her sanity.

"Natasha," Olivia whispered almost silently, "I need you. Please help me."

A single tear started to roll down her cheek.

Chapter 9

Natasha had managed to drag herself to an upright position. Her eyes were becoming accustomed to the dark and she could see there was a deep cut in her hand. She took off one of her socks, slipped her sneaker back on, and wrapped the sock around her hand as best she could. The rats she thought she had heard earlier had either scuttled back into the blackness, or were maybe just small mice, which were no doubt more frightened of her than she was of them. She tried to think. She had absolutely no idea why Ellis was doing this. All she did know was that she had to get out of here, and fast. Who knew what sort of trouble Olivia was in? It was beginning to get even colder in here, there were no windows so no sunlight permeated the room. Then, with a start, Natasha saw the reason for the sudden onset of cold. The slight figure of Suzanna Craigson had appeared in the corner of the room. Natasha limped back in fear until her back was already pressed hard against the wall, and she could move back no further.

"Natasha, please don't be afraid," Suzanna started. She held out her hand towards the terrified girl. "Please, believe me! I'm here to help you. You must get out of here, and quickly. She has Olivia."

"Ellis has Olivia – where?" Natasha asked. She tried to move.

"Oh blast, it," she kicked at the wall in frustration, momentarily forgetting her swollen ankle, and drawing back in pain. "How can I get out of here?" she asked. "There aren't any windows. I can't budge the door. What am I supposed to do?" Somewhere in the back of her rational mind, she was thinking "I'm conversing with a ghost, I've completely lost it now, I'm talking to a ghost."

For now though, rational thoughts took second place to the crisis at hand: getting out of this dark cellar and finding her friend. Suzanna spoke again.

"Natasha, you must listen to me, and listen carefully. I lived in this house once upon a time, and I know the passageways. If you follow my instructions, I can get you out of here, but you must listen very carefully."

Natasha nodded.

"I'm listening," she said.

Suzanna turned towards the wall opposite the door and pointed to a large stone which jutted out more than the others.

"If you press this, it will open out on to a passageway which leads to the kitchens. Just inside the doorway before you proceed down the passage, put your hand in to the left and you will be able to feel a candle and some matches. They have been there since my time in this house, and now you must make use of them."

Suzanna gave more directions as Natasha listened intently, trying vainly to ignore the pain in both her hand and her ankle.

"Quickly, Natasha," Suzanna's figure started to fade. "You must hurry, there's no time to waste."

As the girl disappeared completely from view, Natasha moved towards the stone and pressed hard. As Suzanna had said, the wall began to move, slowly, not having been moved for years, and opened out on to a large passageway. She felt to the left of her, picked up the candle and lit it with a match, then began to limp as fast as she could along the passageway.

The boat was almost a quarter full by now. Olivia was desperately trying not to panic as she knew any movement she made in the boat would merely worsen the situation. Ellis, meanwhile, had resumed her story.

"And so Jemma waited, waited until the Craigsons were out of sight, before she went indoors, discarded her outer garments and went to seek out Suzanna. She found her outside, and

quickly set her plan into action. She invited her
out in the small rowing boat which was always
moored to the side of the small lake and, when
Suzanna showed some fear, for she could not
swim, quickly dispelled her doubts and reassured her that everything would be just fine.
Would she, Jemma, let anything happen to her
dearest friend? Suzanna smiled. She was being
silly, of course. Jemma would take care of her,
hadn't she always?

"The two girls went to the lake and helped
one another into the small rowing boat, each taking hold of a paddle. Jemma started to sing
'Row, row, row your boat,' and Suzanna joined
in, both girls laughing together as they neared
the centre of the lake. Then, just at the centre and
deepest part, Jemma dared Suzanna to stand up,
saying that she also would stand. After some

hesitation the trusting young girl did as she was bid, but when Jemma stood it was to grasp the girl roughly and push her out of the boat and into the dark murky waters. Suzanna bravely tried to fight her off, her eyes wild with both fear and disbelief, but remember she was a slight girl, weakened by illness and her disability, and her strength could not compare with that of Jemma. One final push and she was in the water. Jemma didn't wait to see whether or not her friend's head would bob back up, instead rowing to the other side of the lake as quickly as she could in order to retrieve her dry clothes from the boat house where she had placed them that morning.

Suzanna did surface, at least twice, struggling to breathe, trying to call out for her beloved parents, fighting for her life. The last sight she saw, just before her lungs filled completely with water, was that of her friend clambering from the boat at the lake's edge, and the last emotion she felt was that of betrayal."

"Betrayal, Olivia. Is that what you're feeling now that I've betrayed your friendship? I hope you're feeling that, Olivia, I hope you're feeling terrible, terrible, fear, because you know that I will never help you."

Olivia, crying silently, looked at the girl on the other side of the lake, and said nothing.

Ellis had started to speak again.

"Of course it didn't work," she continued. "The Craigsons were so distraught at the loss of their poor daughter that they couldn't even bear to look at Jemma, she reminded them of Suzanna so much. The final straw came one day, a few weeks later, when Jemma dressed in Suzanna's new dress, the one she was to wear to her fourteenth birthday party, thinking maybe Mr and Mrs Craigson would like to see her wear it, that their hearts would soften would soften maybe when they saw her dressed and looking so beautiful in it. Of course the silly creature only distressed them even more. Mrs Craigson was almost hysterical with grief and Mr Craigson shut himself away in his study. Downstairs, in the kitchens, Ellen chastised her daughter for being so vain and unthinking. She was aware of her daughter's faults, and that the girl could be vain, greedy and spiteful. Although she tried to banish the thought from her mind, she wondered sometimes if Jemma had been in any way involved with the boating accident. The Craigsons' grief was such that she felt like a complete outsider, and that her daughter's presence was a constant reminder to them of Suzanna. She left some weeks later and settled in a town a few hundred miles away. Ellen Goulden – name mean anything to you, Olivia?"

Olivia started. "Goulden – it's a common enough name, Ellis, why should it mean anything to me?"

"Because she was your relation, that's why, Olivia. She wormed her way into poor Suzanna's affections and then disposed of her when she felt like it. Do you know what my mother's maiden name was, Olivia? Craigson. Yes, that's right, Craigson. Suzanna was, or would have been, her great, great grandmother, but your greedy relation decided to snuff out her life, do away with her in order to try and inherit her money. Sad, isn't it, that it didn't work, Olivia. Us Craigsons, though, are made of sterner stuff. Suzanna's father had sisters and brothers scattered throughout the county and one of the younger brothers and his wife came her to Gatesfell to settle, and make sure that the family line was continued. So here I am. And there you are."

Ellis glanced in Olivia's direction. "Not long now," she thought. The boat was just about to topple.

"Olivia, hold on, I'm coming."

Olivia turned in the direction of the voice. Marcie was running towards her with an older man – her father – Olivia later realised. Ellis looked up, dismayed, only to see that Natasha, too, had escaped and was limping towards the lake. Marcie's father though was the one who dived into the lake and swam out towards the almost capsized boat. He was the one who pulled Olivia from the boat and half-dragged, half-swam with her back towards the bank. And he

was the one who held her gently in his arms
while she cried.

Chapter 10

The girls found out the next day that Ellis had rung Marcie at nine o'clock to tell her that the lunch at Gatefells had been cancelled and not to bother coming.

Marcie, however, returned from a shopping trip with her mother and telephoned Natasha to meet up with her that afternoon only to be told by Mrs Morris that Natasha and Olivia were at Gatefells! Never having trusted the girl much, anyway, Marcie suspected something was afoot and asked her father to take her to Ellis's house.

Natasha and Olivia placed small bunches of flowers on the grave and sat quietly for a few moments before getting up to leave the cemetery.

"Goodbye Suzanna," whispered Olivia, "and thanks for everything."

Natasha linked arms with her best and dearest friend.

"What a shame nobody could have saved her in time – guess it just wasn't meant to be," she sighed. "At least we've still got you," she smiled and hugged her friend.

Natasha still limped slightly from her fall in the cellar. The doctor said it was just a very bad sprain and she should rest as much as possible.

"No more hockey for a few weeks," she joked with Olivia.

"What do you think will happen to Ellis, then?" asked Olivia.

"Who knows," Natasha replied. "Probably a remand home or something. No more than she deserves."

Olivia turned to close the gate to the cemetery and noticed one of the graves was strewn with fresh flowers. She raised her eyes to look at the tombstone. There were only two words inscribed there – Jemma Goulden.

We hope you have enjoyed this story from the pen of Edgar J. Hyde. Here are some other titles in the Creepers series for you to collect:

Rag & Bone Man
Payback Time
Cold Kisser
Noisy Neighbours
The Sold Souls

This series was conceived by Edgar J. Hyde and much of the text was provided by his minions, under slavish conditions and pain of death! Thankfully, none of these minions defied their master and so we can say 'thank you' to them for toughing it out and making this series possible.

Edgar J. Hyde, however, has yet more plans for these dungeon-bound slaves. 'No rest for the wicked' is his motto!

Creepers

NOISY NEIGHBOURS

A seemingly puritanically-minded family move to a big run-down area in a big city.

They refuse to talk to their new neighbours as they regard them as inferior. But something doesn't quite fit with this family. At night all the wild, partying noises come from their house and through the blinds, the neighbours see shadows of what looks like inhuman forms.

Killjoys during the day – fun lovers at night, this Jekyll and Hyde type family come under the scrutiny of three teenage would-be ghost busters!

Creepers

PAYBACK
TIME

A family's life is made a misery by loansharks who then discover that they have bitten off more than they can chew. The family pay back the moneylenders in carefully worked out instalments and with interest!

Mysteriously, the family is helped by the sympathetic previous tenant of their home, who was forced out by the same loansharks in the past

This tenant disappeared under unexplained circumstances and now seems to appear only at the moments of most need!

Creepers

RAG & BONE MAN

In a small village the night after every funeral, an apparition of a rag and bone man, with his horse and cart, reputedly makes his way down the high street.

The trouble is, the person reporting the sight is normally the next person in a coffin!

Thus a conspiracy of silence prevails among the locals and the legend remains unconfirmed. Until, after the death of an elderly relative, Bryan Codie and Dave decide to investigate . . .

Creepers

THE
SOLD SOULS

A collection of overambitious high school children who, through dabbling in the occult, sell their souls to a harmless, minor demon who poses as the Devil! They would do anything for success, not knowing that by selling their souls to an impostor, they have incurred the wrath of the real thing!

Now the real Devil gets his own back by posing convincingly as people they know. They are then led, in blissful ignorance to untimely ends.

Will any of them survive?

Creepers

COLD KISSER

All the boys at school want to kiss the new girl until one boy does. Word then gets around about her cold kiss which seemed to freeze him in time, like a temporary kiss of death.

Another boy, Tommy therefore does all he can to resist kissing the new girl, Sally Anne.

Strangely, he feels as if he's known her before. But when and where?